Roses are Red Violets are Blue

AF432381

Roses are Red Violets are Blue

Roses are Red Violets are Blue

Roses are Red Violets are Blue

Roses are Red Violets are Blue

Roses are Red Violets are Blue

Roses are Red Violets are Blue

Roses are Red Violets are Blue

Roses are Red Violets are Blue

Roses are Red Violets are Blue

Roses are Red Violets are Blue

Roses are Red Violets are Blue

Roses are Red Violets are Blue

Roses are Red Violets are Blue

Roses are Red Violets are Blue

Roses are Red Violets are Blue

Roses are Red Violets are Blue

Roses are Red Violets are Blue

Roses are Red Violets are Blue

Roses are Red Violets are Blue

Roses are Red Violets are Blue

Roses are Red Violets are Blue

Roses are Red Violets are Blue

Roses are Red Violets are Blue

Roses are Red Violets are Blue

Roses are Red Violets are Blue

Roses are Red Violets are Blue

Roses are Red Violets are Blue

Roses are Red Violets are Blue

Roses are Red Violets are Blue

Roses are Red Violets are Blue

Roses are Red Violets are Blue

Roses are Red Violets are Blue

Roses are Red Violets are Blue

Roses are Red Violets are Blue

Roses are Red Violets are Blue

Roses are Red Violets are Blue

Roses are Red Violets are Blue

Roses are Red Violets are Blue

Roses are Red Violets are Blue

Roses are Red Violets are Blue

Roses are Red Violets are Blue

Roses are Red Violets are Blue

Roses are Red Violets are Blue

Roses are Red Violets are Blue

Roses are Red Violets are Blue

Roses are Red Violets are Blue

Roses are Red Violets are Blue

Roses are Red Violets are Blue

Roses are Red Violets are Blue

Roses are Red Violets are Blue

Roses are Red Violets are Blue

Roses are Red Violets are Blue

Roses are Red Violets are Blue

Roses are Red Violets are Blue

Roses are Red Violets are Blue

Roses are Red Violets are Blue

Roses are Red Violets are Blue

Roses are Red Violets are Blue

Roses are Red Violets are Blue

Roses are Red Violets are Blue

Roses are Red Violets are Blue

Roses are Red Violets are Blue

Roses are Red Violets are Blue

Roses are Red Violets are Blue

Roses are Red Violets are Blue

Roses are Red Violets are Blue

Roses are Red Violets are Blue

Roses are Red Violets are Blue

Roses are Red Violets are Blue

Roses are Red Violets are Blue

Roses are Red Violets are Blue

Roses are Red Violets are Blue

Roses are Red Violets are Blue

Roses are Red Violets are Blue

Roses are Red Violets are Blue

Roses are Red Violets are Blue

Roses are Red Violets are Blue

Roses are Red Violets are Blue

Roses are Red Violets are Blue

Roses are Red Violets are Blue

Roses are Red Violets are Blue

Roses are Red Violets are Blue

Roses are Red Violets are Blue

Roses are Red Violets are Blue

Roses are Red Violets are Blue

Roses are Red Violets are Blue

Roses are Red Violets are Blue

Roses are Red Violets are Blue

Roses are Red Violets are Blue

Roses are Red Violets are Blue

Roses are Red Violets are Blue

Roses are Red Violets are Blue

Roses are Red Violets are Blue

Roses are Red Violets are Blue

Roses are Red Violets are Blue

Roses are Red Violets are Blue

Roses are Red Violets are Blue

Roses are Red Violets are Blue

Roses are Red Violets are Blue